DISCARD

FCPL discards materials that are outdated and in poor condition. In order to make room for current, in-demand materials, underused materials are offered for public sale.

Artist's Studio
Photography

by Jenny Fretland VanVoorst

Bullfrog Books

Ideas for Parents and Teachers

Bullfrog Books let children practice reading informational text at the earliest reading levels. Repetition, familiar words, and photo labels support early readers.

Before Reading
- Discuss the cover photo. What does it tell them?
- Look at the picture glossary together. Read and discuss the words.

Read the Book
- "Walk" through the book and look at the photos. Let the child ask questions. Point out the photo labels.
- Read the book to the child, or have him or her read independently.

After Reading
- Prompt the child to think more. Ask: Do you like to look at photographs? What sorts of photographs appeal to you? Have you ever taken one yourself?

Bullfrog Books are published by Jump!
5357 Penn Avenue South
Minneapolis, MN 55419
www.jumplibrary.com

Copyright © 2016 Jump! International copyright reserved in all countries. No part of this book may be reproduced in any form without written permission from the publisher.

Library of Congress Cataloging-in-Publication Data

Fretland VanVoorst, Jenny, 1972– author.
  Photography / by Jenny Fretland VanVoorst.
      pages cm. — (Artist's studio)
  Includes index.
  ISBN 978-1-62031-283-4 (hardcover: alk. paper) —
  ISBN 978-1-62496-343-8 (ebook)
  1. Photography—Juvenile literature. I. Title.
  TR149.F88 2015
  770—dc23
                                           2015033392

Series Designer: Ellen Huber
Book Designer: Michelle Sonnek
Photo Researcher: Michelle Sonnek

Photo Credits: All photos by Shutterstock except: iStock, 8, 10; Thinstock, 12, 14–15, 17, 20–21, 22tl, 23tl.

Printed in the United States of America at Corporate Graphics in North Mankato, Minnesota.

Table of Contents

Click!	4
A Photographer's Tools	22
Picture Glossary	23
Index	24
To Learn More	24

Click!

Mel is a photographer.

She takes pictures of places.

She takes pictures of people.

Mel shoots what she sees.

Her photos show how she sees them.

She turns simple moments into art.

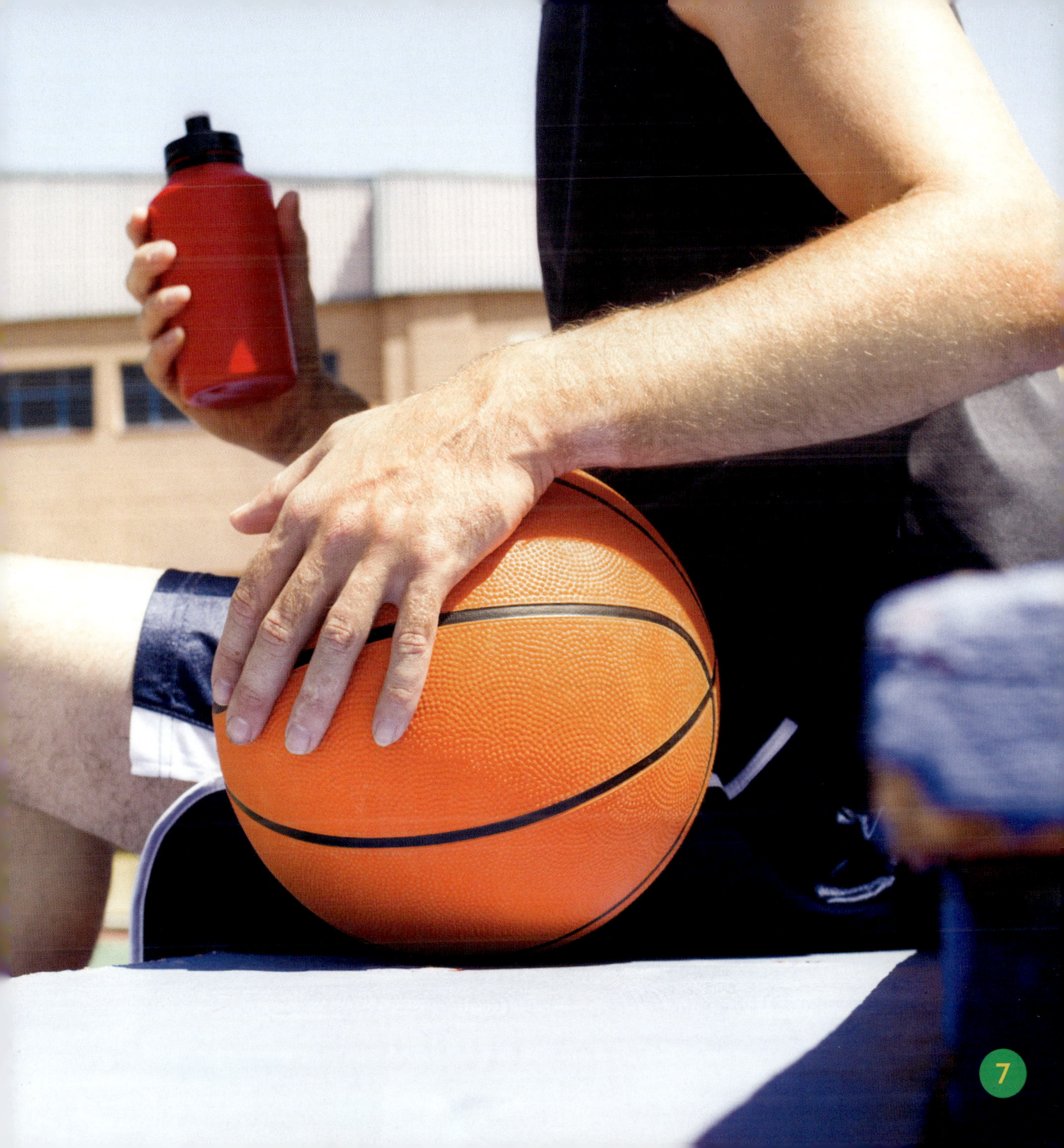

Look! Mel sees two men.
They are playing a game.

She lifts her camera.

10

Click. She takes the shot.

Do you like Mel's picture?

Al is a photographer, too.

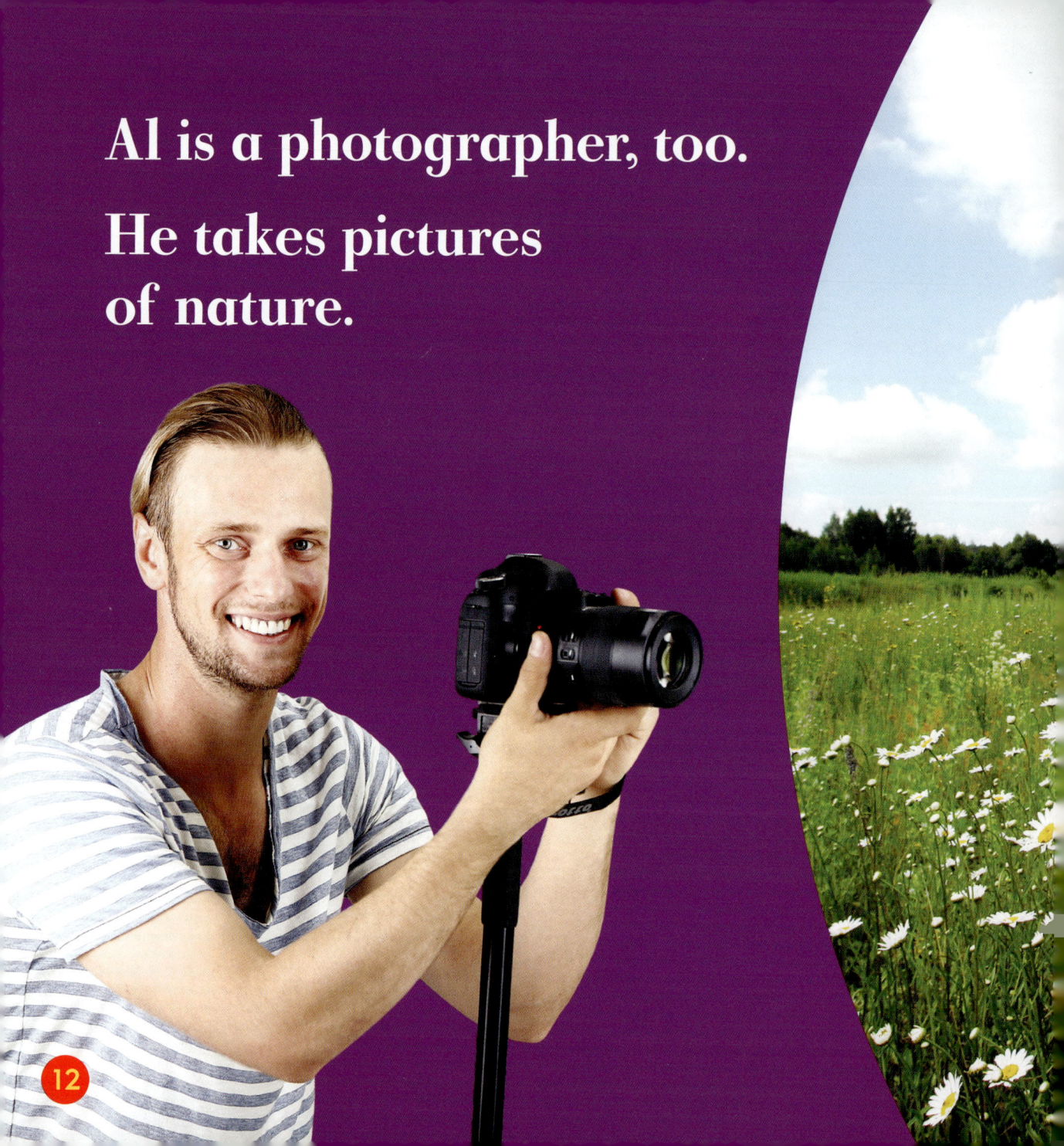

He takes pictures of nature.

13

macro lens

He uses a macro lens.

It makes small things look bigger.

Look!
Al sees a bee.
Shh!

He lifts his camera.

Click. He takes the shot.

Do you like Al's picture?

19

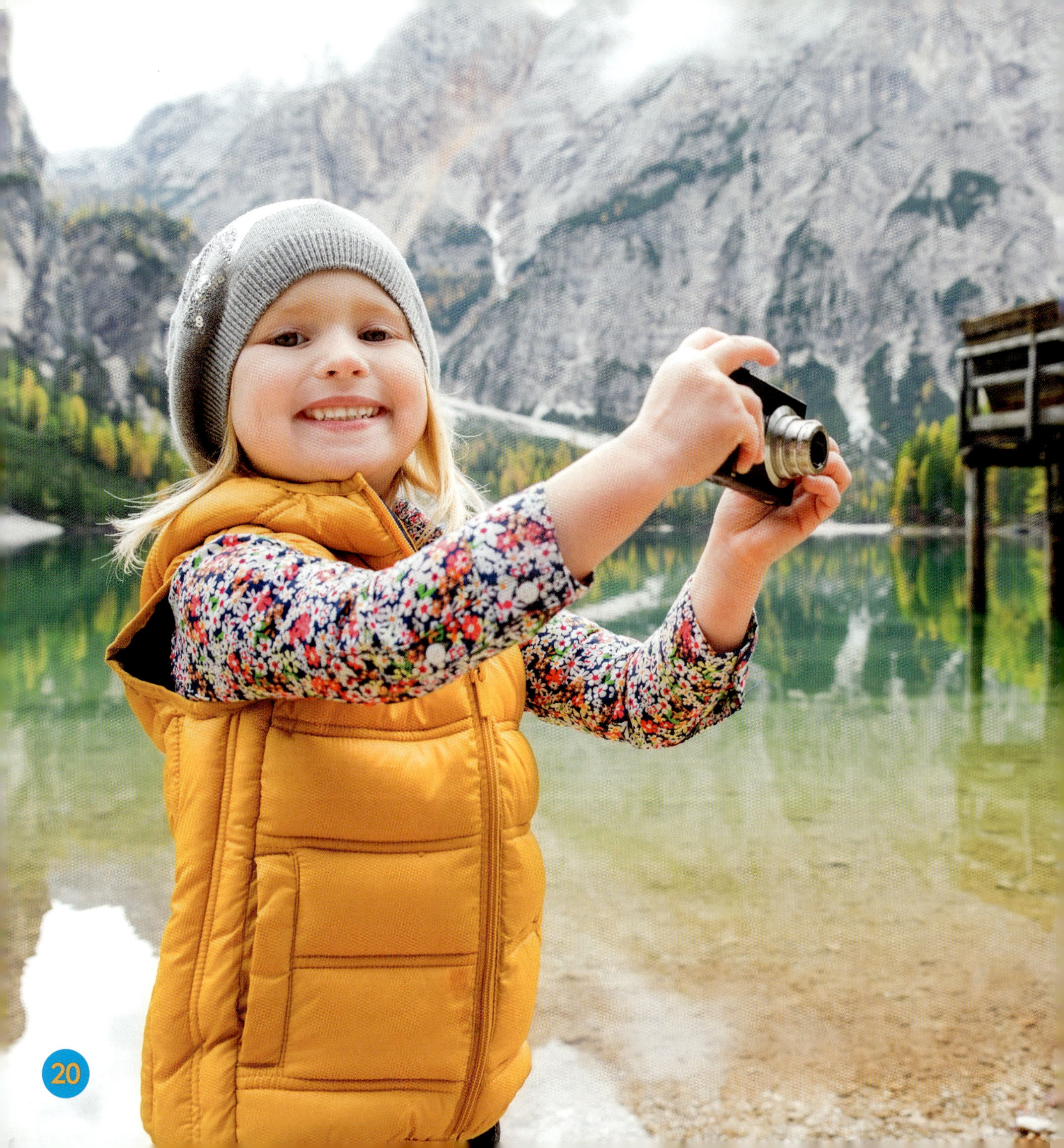

Grab a camera.
Give it a try.
Photography is fun!

A Photographer's Tools

lights

camera

lens

tripod

Picture Glossary

camera
A device that records images.

shoot
To take a picture with a camera.

macro lens
A clear, curved material that bends light to form an image and magnify an object.

shot
A photograph.

Index

art 6
bee 16
camera 9, 17, 21
game 8
macro lens 15
moments 6

nature 12
people 5
photographer 4, 12
pictures 5, 11, 12, 18
places 5
shooting 6, 11, 18

To Learn More

Learning more is as easy as 1, 2, 3.
1) Go to www.factsurfer.com
2) Enter "photography" into the search box.
3) Click the "Surf" button to see a list of websites.

With factsurfer.com, finding more information is just a click away.